OTHER BOOKS FROM KANE/MILLER

One Woolly Wombat
The Magic Bubble Trip
The House From Morning to Night
Wilfrid Gordon McDonald Partridge
Brush
I Want My Potty
Girl From the Snow Country
Cat In Search of a Friend
The Truffle Hunter
Goodbye Rune
The Umbrella Thief

First American Edition 1987 by Kane/Miller Book Publishers
Brooklyn, New York & La Jolla, California

Originally published in England in 1987 by Oxford University Press
Illustrations copyright © Korky Paul 1987
Text copyright © Valerie Thomas 1987

Library of Congress Cataloging-in-Publication Data

Paul, Korky.
  Winnie the witch.
  Summary: Because Winnie the Witch lives in a house
where everything is black, she can not see her black
cat—until she comes up with a brilliant, and colorful,
idea.
  [1. Witches—Fiction. 2. Cats—Fiction] I. Thomas,
Valerie. II. Title.
PZ7.P278348Wi 1987   [E]   87-3612
ISBN 0-916291-13-8

Printed in Hong Kong

1 2 3 4 5 6 7 8 9 10

Winnie the Witch

Korky Paul *and* Valerie Thomas

A CRANKY NELL BOOK

KM Kane/Miller Book Publishers

Brooklyn, New York & La Jolla, California

Winnie the Witch lived in a black
house in the forest.
The house was black on the outside
and black on the inside.
The carpets were black.
The chairs were black.
The bed was black and it had
black sheets and black blankets.
Even the bath was black.

Winnie lived in her black house
with her cat, Wilbur. He was black too.
And that is how the trouble began.

When Wilbur sat on a chair with
his eyes open Winnie could see him.
She could see his eyes, anyway.

But when Wilbur closed his eyes
and went to sleep,
Winnie couldn't see him at all.
So she sat on him.

When Wilbur sat on the carpet
with his eyes open, Winnie could see him.
She could see his eyes anyway.

But when Wilbur closed his eyes
and went to sleep,
Winnie couldn't see him at all.
So she tripped over him.

One day, after a nasty fall, Winnie
decided something had to be done.
She picked up her magic wand,
waved it once and ABRACADABRA!
Wilbur was a black cat no longer.
He was bright green!

Now, when Wilbur slept on a chair,
Winnie could see him.

When Wilbur slept on the floor,
Winnie could see him.

And she could see him when he slept on the bed.
But, Wilbur was not allowed to sleep on the bed . . .

. . . so Winnie put him outside.
Outside in the grass.

Winnie came hurrying outside,
tripped over Wilbur,
turned three somersaults,
and fell into a rose bush.

When Wilbur sat outside in the grass,
Winnie couldn't see him,
even when his eyes were wide open.

This time, Winnie was furious.
She picked up her magic wand,
waved it five times and . . .

. . . ABRACADABRA! Wilbur had a red head,
a yellow body, a pink tail, blue whiskers,
and four purple legs.
But his eyes were still green.

Now, Winnie could see Wilbur when
he sat on a chair, when he lay on the
carpet, when he crawled into the grass.

And even when he climbed to the top of the tallest tree.

Wilbur climbed to the top of the tallest tree to hide.
He looked ridiculous and he knew it.
Even the birds laughed at him.

Next morning Wilbur was
still up the tree.
Winnie was worried.
She loved Wilbur and hated
him to be miserable.

Wilbur was miserable.
He stayed at the top of the tree
all day and all night.

Then Winnie had an idea.
She waved her magic wand and
ABRACADABRA! Wilbur was a
black cat once more.
He came down from the tree, purring.

Then Winnie waved her wand again, and again, and again.

Now instead of a black house,
she had a yellow house with a
red roof and a red door.
The chairs were white with red
and white cushions. The carpet
was green with pink roses.

The bed was blue, with pink and
white sheets and pink blankets.
The bath was a gleaming white.

And now, Winnie can see Wilbur
no matter where he sits.